THE BRITISH EMPIRE, 1837

EQUATOR

Canada
Newfoundland
Bermuda
Bahama Is.
Turks and Caicos Is.
Jamaica
West Indies
British Honduras
Trinidad
British Guiana
Falkland Is.

Shetland
Orkney
Heligoland
Gibraltar
Malta
Ionian Is.
Gambia
Sierra Leone
Gold Coast
India
Ascension I.
EQUATOR
Ceylon
Malay Straits Settlements
St Helena I.
Seychelles
Mauritius
Port Natal
Cape Colony
Swan River Settlement
South Australia
Victoria
New South Wales
Van Diemen's Land
Flinders Island

WALKER ST
ROBERT ST
AGOON RD

...ally accessible bird habitats, ranging
from coastal dunes and cliffs, mountains,
heath, woodland, farms and forest to
extensive wetlands.

About 150 species
recorded from the
including eight of
endemic species.
Forty-spotted Par
the Black (mour
Perhaps the m
Muttonbirds –
which return
millions to t
various sma
The Cape

The Municipality of Flinders
welcomes visitors

...RE ALERT

...n and beautiful

59 2000
59 3506

59 2122
59 2011

Gary Crew & Peter Gouldthorpe
c/o Lothian Books,
11 Munro St,
Port Melbourne
VICTORIA.

3 2 0 7

Geoff Middleton
c/- Post Office
Flinders Island
via Tasmania 7255
15 October 1994

Dear Sirs

Two weeks ago I was in the audience when you
gave a public address on writing and book illustration
at the Flinders Island School Library. What you had
to say interested me very much, and after long
consideration I am writing to present you with a
proposal which you will no doubt find very strange.
I ask you to bear with me.

You mentioned that you had taken time out
from your lecturing schedule to go bushwalking to the
north of Flinders Island, in the vicinity of Mount
Killiecrankie, and that you, Mr Crew, had been
fossicking for some of our famous Killiecrankie diamonds,
while you, Mr Gouldthorpe, had taken the opportunity
of sketching the mountain. It was clear that the
rugged terrain in the region made a lasting impression
on you. It has had the same effect on me.

When I first came to this island nearly thirty years ago, I stumbled upon a story about Mount Killiecrankie that has haunted me to this day. It is a story of terrible loss, not just of enormous wealth but of lives too, including one for which I hold myself responsible. You see, I am no innocent bystander in this tale. For many years I have longed to speak out, to tell the truth, but I lacked the courage. Hearing you lecture the other night – and noting how you spoke of Killiecrankie – I knew that you would listen.

Enclosed are all the materials pertaining to my story. You may think it is no more than the ravings of some madman, hiding out in the wilderness on this God-forsaken island. I could well understand that but, believe me, what I have provided for you is the truth: a terrible untold truth spanning many years and many lives.

I offer this story to you in the hope that you might tell it to the world. I believe it is a story which must be told. Should you choose to do so, I expect no financial reward. I am making a living, such as it is. As for copyright ownership – there is no other claimant; the boy I speak of, Aaron Bates, has long since gone to his people – too soon, as you will see, and to my shame.

If the material is of no use to you, please dispose of it as you see fit. I could not bear to see it again.

Yours sincerely,

Geoff Middleton

Lothian Books

Book Publisher and Distributor A.C.N. 004 064 297
11 Munro Street, Port Melbourne, Victoria 3207 Australia
SAN 900-0313 Telephone (03) 645 1544 Fax (03) 646 4882

11 November 1994

Geoff Middleton
C/- Post Office
Whitemark
Flinders Island 7255

Dear Mr Middleton

Thank you for your letter to Gary Crew and Peter Gouldthorpe, which we forwarded to them on receipt. We have since had their response - an extremely enthusiastic one - and our publishing committee has considered their proposal to produce an illustrated book of your story of the lost Killiecrankie diamonds.

In short, we would very much like to publish it as a hardcover book, with text by Gary and illustrations by Peter, but also with as many of your own materials as are relevant. If you are agreeable, I wonder if you would mind sending us any other photographs, sketches, documents, etc. which relate to the story, or indeed to Flinders Island in general, from which Peter and Gary can make a choice?

I understand that you have given them your written permission to use the materials already sent, and that there are no copyright considerations. We would, of course, acknowledge the use of your materials in the book. We would be grateful if you could check the final text, too, to ensure both that it is accurate and that you are happy with it.

I look forward to your reply, and to working with you on this fascinating project. Gary and Peter both agree that it is, as you say, a story which must be told.

Yours sincerely

Helen Chamberlin

Helen Chamberlin
Senior Editor

Thomas C. Lothian Pty Ltd Inc. in Victoria Est. 1888

This book is dedicated
to the people of Flinders and
Cape Barren Islands,
whose assistance
was greatly appreciated.

With special thanks to Margot Welsh.

A Lothian Book

Thomas C. Lothian Pty Ltd
11 Munro Street, Port Melbourne,
Victoria 3207

First published 1995

National Library of Australia
Cataloguing-in-publication data:

Crew, Gary, 1947–,
The lost diamonds of Killiecrankie

ISBN 0 85091 714 X.

I. Gouldthorpe, Peter. II. Title.

A823.3

Cover and text design by David Salter, Independent Graphic Design
Typeset in Australia by David Salter, Independent Graphic Design
Colour separations by J. Film Process Singapore Pte Ltd

Printed in Australia by Southbank Book

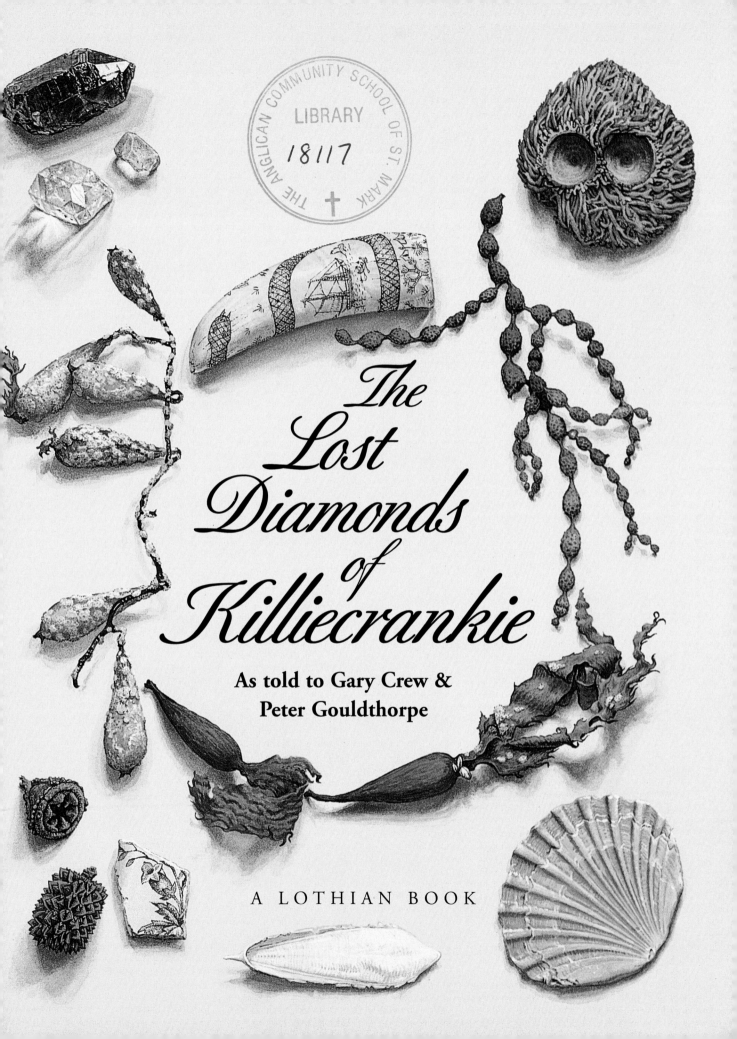

The Lost Diamonds of Killiecrankie

As told to Gary Crew & Peter Gouldthorpe

A LOTHIAN BOOK

The Strzelecki peaks, photograph, P.G.

I first heard the story of the lost diamonds of Killiecrankie from a group of boys I met on Flinders Island, back in March 1969. I was fresh from the Academy of Art and had just started my first job: a six-month contract as an art teacher at a high school in Launceston. This was a big mistake. I had forgotten how much I hated schools. Not the kids – they were fine, in fact I was only a few years older than some of them. It was the routine that I couldn't cope with: the uniformity, the rules, the bells! I gave it my best, I tried to conform, but one Friday morning, three months into my contract, I knew that I had to take a break – for a long weekend, at least.

Some of my artist friends from the Academy had been on a sketching tour of Flinders Island. They were always telling me that it was an artist's paradise: genuine, unspoiled wilderness, and less than an hour from Launceston by light plane. That particular morning I didn't think twice: I telephoned the school to say that I was sick, booked a ticket, stuffed a few essentials in a backpack, bundled up my painting gear, and by midday I was 9,000 feet above Bass Strait.

I will never forget my first sight of Flinders: the turquoise sea, the shimmering gold of the beaches, the haunting grey-green of the bush. But it was the mountains that made me catch my breath. A range of peaks ran the length of the island, as stark and weathered as the fossilised backbone of some prehistoric beast.

'That's Mount Strzelecki beneath us,' the pilot said. 'And up there,' he nodded towards the north, 'that's Mount Killiecrankie, where the diamonds are.' Craning forward, I saw a solitary peak piercing the cloud. I thought that he was kidding about the diamonds – pulling the tourist's leg, as some locals do – but I didn't care. The mountain was amazing: isolated, mysterious, begging to be painted. I could hardly wait.

When we landed I hitched a ride into Whitemark, the main town on the island. My lift dropped me off outside the general store – there was only one – and I took the town in at a glance: a pub, a post office, a service station, and the store; that was all. Undaunted, I picked up my gear and went in. I needed food, a map, and information about transport. The store seemed the best place to start.

The shelves were almost bare, but I managed to find the essentials, including a few cans that weren't rusty, and took them to the counter. The storekeeper had kept his eye on me the whole time. I guessed that he didn't like my long hair – a bit of a fad left over from my Art Academy days – so I made an attempt to explain myself, and my backpack, since he had his eye on that too. I said, 'I'd like to take a look around Mount Killiecrankie. Is there a bus runs up that way?'

'No public transport on this island,' he said, and started adding my bill on an ancient cash register.

This was a real setback. 'Nothing? I can't walk with all this gear.'

He looked up. 'You going after diamonds?'

'Diamonds?' This was the second time I'd heard them mentioned that afternoon. 'I don't know about any diamonds. I'm an artist. I'm here to paint. See?' I undid my pack just enough to give him a glimpse of my easel.

He came around for a closer look. Satisfied, he said, 'You drive a car?'

'Yes.'

'I mean, have you got a driver's licence?'

'Sure.'

'Then I could rent you a vehicle. I got a few next door, at the garage.'

I'd noticed a few beaten-up jalopies in the yard. 'How much?' I said.

'Five bucks a day. You pay the petrol.'

I'd spent my money on the air ticket; besides, the cars weren't worth it. 'I can't afford that,' I said. 'I'll have to walk,' and I started to gather up my groceries.

'Hang on,' he said. 'I've got a push bike. I could let you have that. How long you here for?'

'The weekend.'

'Okay. Say two bucks the weekend for a push bike. Can you afford that?'

'Depends. Will it take all my gear?'

'See for yourself,' he said, and led me into the garage.

Suspended from the wall by a pair of iron hooks was a woman's bike, complete with a woven cane basket fitted to the handle bars and a luggage rack on the back. 'The wife's,' he explained. He reached up and I helped him lift it down. 'She passed away almost a year ago now, but I didn't have the heart to get rid of this. She used it for collecting shells. Paper nautilus wash up on the beach here, thousands of them every winter. She'd load this up,' he touched the front basket, 'and put a carton on the back too. When the shells were cleaned and packed, she'd send them off to the city dealers. Anyway, the bike's yours if you want it. Two bucks, okay?'

'I'll take it,' I said, wheeling it out, 'but I'll need a map. I only saw the mountain from the plane. I don't know how to get there.'

'I got maps, but before I let you go, I'll need some security. Twenty bucks, maybe?'

Did he think that I was going to steal the thing? Where could I take it, for goodness sake? Off the island by submarine? 'I haven't got that much,' I admitted.

He scratched his chin. 'You got your driver's licence on you? Okay. Leave it with me, and the bike's yours.'

I rested the bike against the front of the shop, took out my wallet and meekly handed over my licence.

'Middleton,' he muttered, reading my name. 'Geoffrey John Middleton. We had a preacher here called Middleton once. Caused a hell of a lot of trouble. Stirred up the natives, no end.' He studied my face, waiting for a response.

So far as I knew, all the Tasmanian Blacks had died out a century ago. 'No relation,' I said, evading the issue.

He grunted and slipped my licence into his wallet. Next thing he gave me a gap-toothed grin and extended his hand. 'Bowman's the name. Lex Bowman. Now, let's get you paid up, packed and away.'

This was my first encounter with an islander. They had strange ways, as I was to learn.

It was mid-afternoon by the time I left Bowman's store. The sun was bright, the road north clear and straight, the landscape an artist's delight. I could feel myself recharging with every mile, but by five-thirty common sense told me to watch out for a place to spend the night. There were plenty of tracks leading off to my left, and I chose one at random, excited by the prospect of setting up camp in some dunes or among the granite boulders that littered the shore. But this was not to be; my education on the true nature of the island was about to begin.

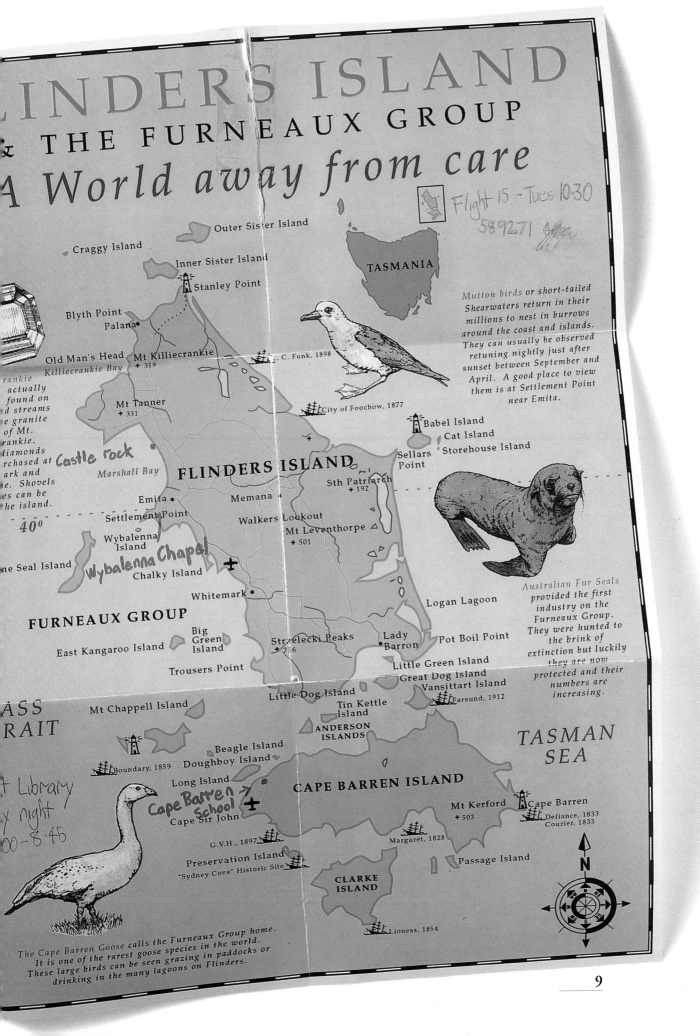

LINDERS ISLAND
& THE FURNEAUX GROUP
A World away from care

Flight 15 - Tues 10:30
589271

Outer Sister Island

Craggy Island

Inner Sister Island

TASMANIA

Stanley Point

Blyth Point
Palana

Old Man's Head
Killiecrankie Bay

Mt Killiecrankie
+ 319

C. Funk, 1898

Mutton birds or short-tailed Shearwaters return in their millions to nest in burrows around the coast and islands. They can usually be observed retuning nightly just after sunset between September and April. A good place to view them is at Settlement Point near Emita.

rankie
actually
found on
d streams
e granite
of Mt.
rankie.
diamonds
rchased at
ark and
e. Shovels
es can be
he island.

Mt Tanner
+ 331

City of Foochow, 1877

Babel Island
Cat Island
Storehouse Island

Castle rock

Marshall Bay

FLINDERS ISLAND

Sth Patriarch
+ 192

Sellars
Point

Emita
Settlement Point

Memana

Walkers Lookout

Mt Leventhorpe
+ 501

40°

Wybalenna
Island

Wybalenna Chapel

Chalky Island

ne Seal Island

Australian Fur Seals provided the first industry on the Furneaux Group. They were hunted to the brink of extinction but luckily they are now protected and their numbers are increasing.

Whitemark

Logan Lagoon

FURNEAUX GROUP

East Kangaroo Island

Big
Green
Island

Strzelecki Peaks
+ 756

Lady
Barron

Pot Boil Point

Trousers Point

Little Green Island
Great Dog Island
Vansittart Island

**ASS
RAIT**

Mt Chappell Island

Little Dog Island

Tin Kettle
Island

Earsund, 1912

**ANDERSON
ISLANDS**

**TASMAN
SEA**

Boundary, 1859

Beagle Island
Doughboy Island

Long Island

Cape Barren
School

CAPE BARREN ISLAND

Mt Kerford
+ 503

Cape Barren

t Library
y night
00 - 8·45

Cape Sir John

G.V.H., 1897

Defiance, 1833
Courier, 1833

Margaret, 1828

Preservation Island
"Sydney Cove" Historic Site

Passage Island

**CLARKE
ISLAND**

N

Lioness, 1854

The Cape Barren Goose calls the Furneaux Group home. It is one of the rarest goose species in the world. These large birds can be seen grazing in paddocks or drinking in the many lagoons on Flinders.

No sooner had I turned than I was struck full on by the wind off the sea, the notorious 'Roaring Forties' that sweep along the 40th parallel from the vast, uncharted regions of the Southern Ocean to batter the western shores of Flinders. I had no hope of riding into it, and dismounted, walking the bike with my head bent and my shoulders hunched.

As I came closer to the sea, the scrub cleared and a grassed valley dotted with sheep appeared before me. The wind was terrible. Some sheep took refuge behind a barn – the only building that I could see – and others rested in the lee of a walled enclosure; a cemetery, I guessed, judging from a headstone that rose above the surrounding wall.

I pushed on, cursing through clenched teeth, any bright ideas of camping by the sea long gone. What I had taken for a barn was a run-down shearing shed of brick and galvanised iron. Wads of greasy fleece littered the floor, wisps of cobwebbed scourings drifted among the rafters and, oddly, at one end, I noticed the remains of a hearth. Was this the shearers' quarters? Did they sleep here too? It was a strange, unsettling place, but it kept the worst of the wind out.

Sketch of Wybalenna, pencil, G.M.

I hauled the bike inside and unrolled my sleeping bag in a corner. I looked at my collection of cans and considered the possibilities for dinner – thanks to Bowman's I could have baked beans straight up or with ham. I decided not to think about it. Whatever the menu, I was freezing, and could do with a fire. Alongside the cemetery was a clump of thorn bushes, their trunks bent low by the constant pressure of the wind. I was certain to find good kindling there – and maybe even a log to throw on after, for company.

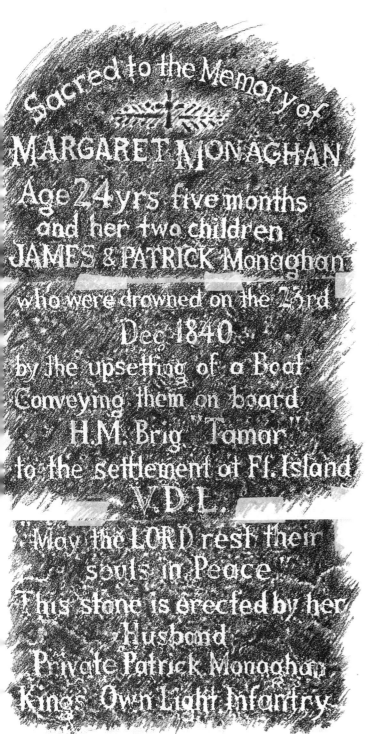

Sacred to the Memory of
MARGARET MONAGHAN
Age 24 yrs five months
and her two children
JAMES & PATRICK Monaghan
who were drowned on the 23rd
Dec 1840
by the upsetting of a Boat
Conveying them on board
H.M. Brig "Tamar"
to the settlement of Ft. Island
V.D.L.
"May the LORD rest their
souls in Peace."
This stone is erected by her
Husband
Private Patrick Monaghan
Kings Own Light Infantry

Headstone at Wybalenna, rubbing, P.G.

I had gathered one load and was returning for another when I noticed the headstone. Earlier it had looked like a lump of grey granite, but now, in the twilight, it glowed crimson and gold. Fascinated by the change, and curious to know more of the life it celebrated, I entered the cemetery enclosure.

The headstone was in a corner, hard against the wall and partly surrounded by a paling fence, long since collapsed. The names of the interred were difficult to read, no doubt having suffered from years of exposure to the elements but, so far as I could tell, the stone marked the final resting place of a young mother and her two infant sons, all three drowned while attempting to disembark from the island, not far from where I stood. I was amazed by this: a boat taking on passengers in this place? I looked beyond the wall. If there had been a dock, or a wharf, where were their remains? Apart from the shed there was no sign of a building. Besides, what lunatic would dare dock here? The sea was a maelstrom; I could hear its dreadful roaring 100 metres away.

I turned, hoping to find some answer on the other tombstones, only to be confronted by a field of grass. There was not a cross, nor a mound, nor any suggestion that this stretch of turf had ever been turned. Had all this land been set aside for three bodies only – so deliberately crowded into a corner – and doubly fenced, at that? A shiver passed over me. What had happened here? What was this awful place?

That night I slept fitfully, listening to the wind howling outside and watching the embers in the long-abandoned fireplace flare and fade as gust after gust invaded my hide-away.

First thing next morning I set out on a leisurely ride north, interrupted only when I was run off the road by some idiot boys who appeared out of nowhere, skylarking on motor bikes. By ten o'clock I had caught sight of Killiecrankie, rising out of the scrub to the west. I stopped and consulted my map. So far as I could make out, I was very near the turn-off which led directly to my goal. This spurred me on, and soon I was negotiating the narrowest of bush tracks, while the looming presence of the mountain occupied more and more of my view.

By midday, the track had petered out among scattered boulders and the bike could go no further. I hid it in a thicket and began to explore on foot.

The mountain was all that I had hoped for: a monolith of weathered granite, the result of some ancient, submarine upheaval, I assumed. The lower areas were dotted with tufts of grass or thick with clumps of tea-tree and she-oak; higher, clear of the protection of the scrub, gnarled and wind-beaten eucalyptus sprang from crevices in the sheer cliffs, drawing sustenance from heaven knows what source.

I was eager to get on with some painting and looked for the best place to set up my easel. I finally chose a clearing that gave me a view of one of the most spectacular outcrops of granite, and returned to collect my gear from the bike. As I dragged it from beneath the bushes, I was certain that I heard whispering. I straightened up and looked around, listening. Had I heard human voices, or simply the wind worrying the grass? Convincing myself that I was still spooked from my experience of the night before, I wheeled the bike to the spot I had chosen and set up my easel.

I worked well for an hour or so, mostly experimenting with sketches in charcoal and crayon until finally deciding that watercolour was the right medium to use, but I had hardly begun when something hit my paper from above. I looked down, trying to find whatever it was. The ground was strewn with a dozen possibilities, from sticks to seeds. I let it pass, but when it happened a second time and then a third, I guessed what was going on. Pretending to take no notice, I waited, then looked up suddenly, just in time to see three boys peering over a ledge 4 or 5 metres away.

I dropped my brush and took off after them. I was fit in those days, and fast on my feet. As I darted through the boulders I heard cries of alarm, and an attempt to start an engine, but I was too quick. Two of the boys were already mounted on their motor bikes when I found them. The third, the smallest of the three, was just about to climb on behind when I grabbed his collar and turned him to face me.

'What the hell do you think you're doing?' I yelled. 'One of those rocks could have killed me.'

The other two dismounted and came to the rescue. 'Aaron done ya no harm,' the biggest protested. 'It was me and Johnno was chuckin' the rocks.'

'Don't give me that,' I said. 'You're all in it together. You're those motor bike hoons who tried to run me off the road this morning. You've been tracking me, haven't you?' I turned my attention to Aaron, the little one. 'As for you, do your parents know where you are?'

'Granite Monoliths', watercolour, G.M.

I used my nastiest teacher voice, hoping to scare him, but his dark eyes stared straight back into mine without a hint of fear. This kid was tough, that was for sure.

'I already told ya to get off his back,' the biggest boy cut in. 'He lives with his grandma. 'Cause his mum and dad was drowned, weren't they, here in the bay.'

Before I could reply, the second boy joined in. 'Yeah, and Aaron doesn't even own a bike, anyway. It's only me and Luke owns bikes. Aaron, he's only got a pony, see? So leave him right out of this, OK?'

I felt terrible. I knew that they were in the wrong but somehow they had managed to make me feel guilty. I muttered something about being sorry – for what, I wasn't sure – and offered a lame warning about behaving more responsibly in the future. At this the two bigger boys turned back to their bikes, considering the show was over, but Aaron held his ground, still staring.

'Go on,' I said, shooing him away. 'Get out of here.'

He did exactly the opposite. He took a step towards me. I thought at first that he was going to give me a mouthful of cheek, but he said, 'Are you an artist?'

'I might be,' I said, my defences still up.

Photograph, G.M.

Luke, Johnno and Aaron lurking in the shadows

He took this in, looked about, looked back at me, then said, 'Are you painting this mountain?' On the word, 'mountain', he opened his arms as if he held the place; as if for a moment, he weighed it in his hands.

'Yes,' I said, 'I am.' I was warming to this kid.

He came closer. 'You reckon I could see what you've done?'

I glanced across at the other two, who had smiles from ear to ear. 'Sure,' I said, 'so long as you don't laugh at it – or chuck rocks. Okay?'

Ten minutes later the four of us were sitting around my easel swigging the last of my precious coke and exchanging life stories.

The biggest boy was Luke, who was fourteen; the next, Johnno, thirteen; and the little one was Aaron Bates, twelve – but 'nearly thirteen', he assured me. When I asked what they were doing on the mountain, apart from tormenting me, Luke answered right away. 'We came up after diamonds,' he said. 'There's still a few in the gullies, if you can get to them.'

I looked from face to face. The diamond thing again. Were they still having a go at me, the wet-behind-the-ears tourist, or were they serious? 'Diamonds?' I said, remaining cautious. 'What? Around here?'

'Killiecrankie diamonds.' Johnno piped up. 'That's what we call them. But they're not really diamonds, they're topaz. Gem-quality topaz. Show him, Luke.'

His friend took a handful of tiny, semi-transparent stones from the pocket of his jeans. 'That's what we found today. They're not too good, these ones, which is how come we was chuckin' them at ya. But if it's cut proper, a good one will knock your eye out sparklin'. My mum's got one like that. Square cut. The size of a stamp. No kidding.'

'And you find them here, on the mountain?'

'Sure. Mixed up with the gravel in gullies up on top. Or in the bay. There's plenty left in the bay.'

'What? On the beach?'

The boys looked towards Aaron. This was obviously his area. 'Under the water,' he said. 'You dive for them. Or pump them up. That's how my mum and dad died. They were out off the point there, off Killie Castle, and this freak wave came in. That was it ...'

Johnno heard him falter and took over. 'There's clear and yellow and pink and blue, but the blue's pale, real pale ...'

'And green,' Luke broke in. 'They reckon someone found green. One time ...' As he spoke Aaron turned, giving him a look. Luke stopped, embarrassed.

Something strange was going on, I could tell. 'You can't leave it like that,' I coaxed. '"One time" what? Tell me.'

'Come on, Aaron,' Johnno agreed. 'He's all right. Tell him the story.'

Luke regained his lost confidence. 'Yeah, Aaron. He's just a tourist. It's not like he'll be comin' back with all his arty-farty mates from the mainland. They wouldn't want to get their hands dirty, hey?'

In spite of Luke's attempt at humour, Aaron wasn't happy. 'There's this stupid story about a green topaz,' he said. 'Sometimes, when we've got nothing else to do, we come up here looking for it. It's just a game, that's all.'

Luke and Johnno exchanged glances. Finally, Johnno took the initiative. 'It's a lot more than that. I know Aaron doesn't like it, but I might as well tell ya, since it was my big mouth started this in the first place.'

Aaron gave him another look, but he went on. 'About 150 years ago this island was used as a dumping ground for Blacks from Tasmania. Tasmanian Aborigines, I mean, right? They lived at a place called Wybalenna – that means "Black Man's Houses". It's about halfway between here and Whitemark. It's a horrible, cold place, windy as hell. Anyway, these poor Blacks, they couldn't take it, see, and nearly all of them died and got chucked in the graveyard there. Hundreds of them, they reckon. All in these unmarked graves ...'

'Not that cemetery near the shearing shed?'

'Yeah, that's the one. That's Wybalenna.'

'I slept there last night. In that shed.'

'Wasn't always a shearing shed.' Aaron's voice was very soft. 'Used to be a church. The white bosses made them go. They didn't even believe in that god.'

It was Johnno's turn to give Aaron the eye. 'So they died, see, these Blacks, and the couple that was left, well, they got shifted back to Tasmania – but there was something they knew about this place, see, something the white man wanted. Wanted real bad. They reckon you could pick diamonds up off the ground in those days. Unbelievable, hey? But the story goes that these Blacks knew where there were real beauties. Green ones. Like emeralds, see? They reckon some Blacks found some, but they disappeared. Poof – you know, vanished. But people say they could still be here; right here, buried right under us.'

The boys left soon after. I walked them to their bikes and they roared off through the scrub, Luke and Johnno yelling promises to return. Unlike the others, Aaron made no promises, but turned back silently, and gave me one last look. I've grappled with that look for nearly forty years. It carried the unspoken certainty that we would meet again.

As luck would have it – or fate, whichever you choose to believe in – I went down sick with a chest infection as soon as I arrived home. For days I drifted in and out of feverish sleep; I lost all interest in food, in friends, even in art. My palette remained untouched. As for school, I phoned in sick daily, then every other day, but as time passed I realised that I simply couldn't face it and neglected to report in at all. I received a few phone calls from my principal, concerned at first, then demanding – followed by a couple of official letters warning me of the consequences if my absence continued.

At the end of three weeks, the big one came.

The Director
Secondary Education
Department of Education
GPO Box 57LHS
HOBART
7001

14 April 1969

Attention: Mr Geoffrey Middleton

Re: Termination of part-time teaching contract

Dear Mr Middleton

Further to departmental memos (Dept of Ed: 368#, 30 March; Dept of
Ed: 404#, 7 April) regarding your continued and unexplained absence
from part-time teaching duties (Art) at Launceston State High School,
I wish to inform you that retrospective to Friday, 10 March, your
teaching contract with this department has been terminated.

Income earned by you during the period 26 January to 10 March will be
paid in full.

The department regrets that this action has been considered
necessary.

Yours sincerely

P. Hockstedder M.A.,B.Ed
DIRECTOR OF SECONDARY EDUCATION.

18

Through all this I had not been able to put Flinders out of my mind. I can't say that the loss of my job really worried me; I was never cut out to be a teacher. When my pay came through I would have returned to the island right away, except my doctor advised me against it, believing that my exposure to the wind there had probably contributed to my infection anyway.

But I didn't forget the place; far from it. One afternoon, as I was moping around my flat, I found myself looking up 'topaz' in an encyclopaedia that I hadn't touched since I was at school. There, staring me in the face, was a reference to the story of the green topaz; those elusive 'diamonds' that the boys had told me about on the island.

Topaz (upper right), smoky quartz (black) and feldspar crystals as they occur in granite pegmatites.
This fine specimen is from Flinders Island, Tasmania.

(Modern Australian Encyclopaedia, *McCoppin Press, Sydney, 1956*)

TOPAZ

Probably from the Sanskrit word *tapas*, meaning 'fire'. A fluorosilicate of aluminium which occurs in association with highly acidic igneous rocks such as granite. It may also be found as water-worn 'pebbles' in alluvial deposits along creek beds or beneath the sea.

The crystal system of topaz is orthorhombic; that is, all angles are right-angles and axes of varying lengths. The stone is hard: 8.5 on the Mohs Scale (diamond is 10; glass 5.5). Stones containing no gas or liquid bubbles usually cut well to form high quality faceted gemstones of varying shapes and sizes.

Most stones are colourless, and as such are often mistaken for diamonds. Such a mistake occurred in the case of the Braganza 'diamond', a clear sparkling stone of 640 carats which was set in the Portuguese crown and believed to be the biggest diamond in the world. It has since been confirmed that this stone is a topaz. Not all topaz are clear, however; yellow (straw-coloured), pale pink and pale blue are sometimes found. During the 1860s it was claimed that a green form of the stone had been found on Mount Killiecrankie, Flinders Island, off the coast of Tasmania. Being a colour variant, the commercial value of such a rare stone would be limitless, far in excess of a diamond of a similar carat. Unfortunately, no green topaz has ever been publicly displayed and experts doubt the possibility of its existence.

YELLOW TOPAZ

PINK TOPAZ

BLUE TOPAZ

Brilliant   Cushion   Pendeloque   Step   Step   Mixed

Call me perverse if you like, but by their very denial those words confirmed for me some peculiar knowledge, some truth as yet untold, that I had already witnessed in the eyes of Aaron Bates.

From that day, I set about preparing for my return to Flinders. Nothing else mattered. I spent every available moment learning all that I could about the island: its geography, its history, its people. I researched in libraries; I sketched in galleries and museums; I sought out private collections of tattered, musty letters, their yellowed pages scribbled in the crabbed and crooked calligraphy of persons long since dead. I could not find enough and the more I found, the more I grew convinced of the existence of those fabulous jewels whose haunting secret, long untold, had already begun to shape my life.

Truganini (died 1876) and William Lanney (died 1869) were believed to be the last female and male of their entire race. Unfortunately, even after death, they were not able to avoid the indignities they had endured in life. Lanney's grave was robbed and Truganini's skeleton became a museum exhibit.

From P. O'Brien, The Last of the Tasmanians, Thomas Carlisle Publishing, Melbourne, 1958

Many people believe that the Tasmanian Aborigine is extinct. Some might recognise a faded photograph of Truganini – whose body was removed from its secret burial place, whose skeleton was wired for public display – and say, 'She was the last Tasmanian female'. A few might even know of William Lanney – whose head, hands and feet were cut off, whose skin was made into a tobacco pouch – and say, 'He was the last Tasmanian male'. All would believe a lie.

While it is true that native Tasmanians were murdered by marauding sealers in the 1790s, were hunted like animals during the notorious 'Black Line' campaign of the 1830s, and were exhumed and dismembered in the 1870s by ghoulish doctors who considered them the much sought-after 'missing link', they survived. But only just.

Through one of history's marvellous ironies, the Tasmanians' greatest threat was not the brutal sealer, nor the soldier, nor the land-grabbing pastoralist, nor the amoral scientist, but the do-gooding Victorian missionary who, given half a chance, would turn the natives into white people – even if they died in the process. The worst of these was George Augustus Robinson (1788–1866), founder of 'Wybalenna', the infamous Aboriginal settlement on Flinders Island.

George Robinson was an English bricklayer who came to Van Diemen's Land in 1824 to better his social standing. He bought a house in Hobart and established his family there, then, hearing that the government was handing out free land (Aboriginal land, that is), he lined up for a few hundred acres on Bruny Island. It was here that he first came in contact with the native population, the young Truganini included, and formed his purpose to 'help' them. He was soon appointed as 'Conciliator and Protector of Aborigines' at a salary of 100 pounds a year.

Robinson was a typical Victorian do-gooder. Show him a black man and he had to save him. Civilise him. Christianise him. Turn him into the only human being the white man considered worthwhile: himself.

With his heart filled with missionary zeal and his pockets lined with government money, Robinson set about gathering the remnants of the

'Natives of Van Diemen's Land', Atlas Australes, *Editions anthropologiques, Paris, 1823, Vol. II*

Aboriginal tribes. From 1828 until 1835 he travelled the length and breadth of Tasmania, using every means possible to lure them – and later force them – to follow him to the 'greener pastures' of various settlements that he had set up for their welfare and protection. Of course, all such establishments were off the main island, separated from whites by the protective boundary of the sea while also serving to prevent escape, should any of the natives be foolhardy enough to try returning to the land of their birth. Bruny Island was considered, then Maria Island, then Swan Island, then Gun Carriage Island – where they were dumped for a while – until finally they ended up at Wybalenna, Flinders Island.

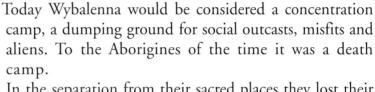

Today Wybalenna would be considered a concentration camp, a dumping ground for social outcasts, misfits and aliens. To the Aborigines of the time it was a death camp.

In the separation from their sacred places they lost their soul.

In the confines of the Christian Church they lost their spirit.

In the forced management of their European crops they lost the right to hunt.

In the draughty little English cottages they lost their health, coughing blood.

In eating the salt-impregnated food rations they lost their fertility.

In Robinson's substitution of their native names with pompous European titles, they lost their identity. Truganini became 'Lalla Rookh'; Woorraddy 'Count Alpha'; Tongerlonster – the once proud chief of the Oyster Bay Tribe – became 'King William'.

But not all was taken lying down. The natives resisted, both actively and passively. They ran away to hunt. They refused to give up their dogs. They continued their 'pagan' dancing. They rejected white man's learning in every form – except when it might be used to their advantage, as when they wrote to the highest authority in the Empire, Queen Victoria, asking that they be free to live independently of the supervisory white man.

Her Majesty was 'pleased to receive' their petition and passed it on to her secretary of state.

Jean-Claude Rival

'George Robinson welcomes natives to Wybalenna' (detail), Benjamin Deveraux, oils
Truganini is to the right, the chapel behind.

When Robinson began his 'round-up' in 1828, there were 500 Aboriginal Tasmanians. By 1847, when Wybalenna was abandoned, forty-seven survivors were returned to the main island: fifteen men, twenty-two women and ten children.

Hidden from society in the derelict, mosquito-infested convict quarters of Oyster Cove, south of Hobart, they dutifully died. Some from malnutrition. Some from alcohol. Some from broken hearts.

But they did not die out. Among the islands of Bass Strait they survived – as whalers' women; as sealers' women, as mutton-birders' women – bearing children and raising them, never once forgetting their Aboriginal identity, never once forfeiting their claim to those islands whose isolation had protected them from Robinson's all-encompassing net.

Now here is a strange thing.

The very same ruffians Robinson would have saved his black disciples from proved to be their Messiahs. Where the social climbing do-gooder had failed, the social misfits succeeded.

Such are the ways of history.

Tasmanian Aborigines at Government House, Hobart, about 1865. William Lanney is on the left, Truganini far right. At the time they were considered to be the last of their race. Photograph: Chas. Woolley, courtesy of Hind-Sight, Tasmania.

'The Freak', oils, artist unknown

While I could find plenty of information on the fate of the Tasmanians exiled to Wybalenna, I could find almost nothing about the topaz, and certainly no historical background. Then one day as I was browsing, I stumbled on a book called *Mission to the Islands,* the memoirs of Canon Marcus Brownrigg, a Church of England missionary who had visited his far-flung flock of Bass Strait islanders in his plucky little sailing vessel, the *Freak.*

In 1872 Brownrigg anchored off Flinders Island to break bread with Mr Peter Gardner, the lessee of Robinson's abandoned settlement at Wybalenna. When spiritual considerations were over, Gardner gave his guest a tour of what remained of the settlement, which Brownrigg later recorded:

> It would be difficult to conceive of a more weird, melancholy, and desolate scene than that which now meets the eye. The buildings are a mere heap of

ruins. The Superintendent's quarters are almost incapable of repair. The brick church, so far as the interior is concerned, is in a pitiable condition, and is used as a shearing shed. The state of the burial ground is truly deplorable. No vestige of any fence remains. The graves are scarcely distinguishable ... Before leaving ... Mr Gardner showed us some specimens he had collected of the very beautiful gems known as 'Killiecrankie Diamonds', and of which he kindly gave us several. Among the specimens in his possession, obtained near the Settlement, we saw one which had been cut and polished in Melbourne. It sparkled very brilliantly, and so nearly resembled the true diamond that none but an experienced lapidary could have detected the difference. Glass may be readily cut with these diamonds. Strictly speaking, however, these gems are not diamonds, but topaz, of which there are here found three varieties – white, yellow, and pink. It is said that the Aborigines at Flinders Island collected 300 specimens of the white topazes, 40 of the yellow, and 30 of the pink, and in addition 30 of the rock crystal, and 30 of beryls, all of which were exhibited at the Crystal Palace in 1851 and attracted great admiration.

This was the first historical reference to the topaz that I had discovered, but it was fraught with problems. There had been no Aborigines on Flinders since 1847, when Wybalenna was abandoned, so who were the 'Aborigines of Flinders Island' who had gathered the gems exhibited in 1851? And what of the green topaz? If it existed, why had Brownrigg mentioned only white, yellow and pink? Was the green stone no more than a beryl? Worse, was it common quartz?

I could not bear to think so and set about inventing theories to convince myself otherwise. For example: if Gardner knew the green diamonds existed or, more likely, had some in his possession, why should he tell Brownrigg? It was one thing to give a visitor a few low-grade, uncut stones – the Flinders boys had done as much for me – but quite another to reveal all; to publicly open the Aladdin's Cave, so to speak, where the most precious gems were hidden.

I focused my research on finding out how and when the gems for the Exhibition of 1851 had been supplied, hoping that the solution to this conundrum may provide some insight into the greater mystery. From my studies at the Art Academy I knew that the Great Exhibition, as it was originally called, was the brain-child of Prince Albert, husband of Queen Victoria. Albert's intention was to find a means of demonstrating the British Empire's cultural and technological superiority over every other nation on Earth. In order to achieve this, the colonies were invited to submit outstanding items of industry or the arts for general admiration, the entire display being mounted in Hyde Park, London. The building itself was modelled on the design of a horticultural hothouse, an architectural triumph of prefabricated iron trusses and glass, the thousands of panes twinkling in the sun. Hence the building's popular title, the 'Crystal Palace'.

'Opening of Crystal Palace', after the style of Sir Thomas Botham R.A., watercolour and ink, 1851

Queen Victoria herself attended Opening Day, on 1 May 1851. It was an occasion of great pomp and ceremony. Victoria writes in her personal journal that she 'wore a dress of pink and silver, with a diamond-ray diadem and little crown at the back with two feathers, all the rest of my jewels being diamonds.' I was struck by this mention of her jewels, but it was nothing compared with the gifts that her subjects lavished on her to celebrate the opening:

> I include a list of the beautiful and interesting things offered for my acceptance, which are of immense value ... The jewels are truly magnificent. The very large pearls, 224 in number, strung in 4 rows, are quite splendid and a very beautiful ornament. The girdle of 19 emeralds is wonderful and also of immense value. The emeralds, square in shape and very large, are alternately engraved ... They are set with diamonds and fringed with pearls. The rubies are even more wonderful ... The one is the largest in the world ... I am very happy that the British Crown will possess these Jewels, for I shall certainly make them Crown Jewels.

And then the trail ran cold.

In the archives of the Colonial Museum, Launceston, I uncovered the official catalogue of the Great Exhibition, and there, in black and white, was the verification of Brownrigg's journal entry – not exactly as he had stated – but near enough to put paid to my search:

Supplied to the Great Exhibition from Van Diemen's Land:

topaz, straw coloured ...	300 pieces from Flinders Island
topaz, yellow	...	40 pieces from Flinders Island
topaz, pink	...	30 pieces no locality stated
beryl [aquamarine]	...	30 pieces no locality stated

There was no mention of green topaz. I felt deflated. Duped. I had swallowed the boys' story hook, line and sinker. What was I, after all, but some arty-farty tourist? I imagined them laughing as they revved their bikes and rode away. I decided then and there to put the entire episode out of my mind.

◆ AN UNEXPECTED LETTER ◆

In the weeks that followed I set about putting my life in order. The first thing I needed was a job. I had relied on social security since losing my teaching contract, and finding work as an artist wasn't exactly easy. I settled for anything. I put in some time as a nurseryman; I helped out at a drycleaner's; I even toughened myself up with some road maintenance for a while – but nothing worthwhile turned up and I was beginning to despair that it ever would, until one afternoon, after a lousy day digging ditches, I came back to the flat to find a peculiar letter buried among the usual pile of bills.

COLONIAL MUSEUM
WELLINGTON STREET
LAUNCESTON
TASMANIA
7250

23 May 1969

Dear Mr Middleton,

Our records show that in April this year you lodged a request with our Information Service for information about Tasmania's contribution to The Great Exhibition of 1851.

The enclosed document was located in our archives. Our Chief Archivist advises that further material relevant to your research topic is held in the State Archives, Hobart. The Museum is happy to retrieve these documents at your request, although the search process may take some time.

If you wish to pursue this issue, a fee for postage and packaging of the said documents will apply.

We await your further advice.

Yours sincerely

Lucy Oliver

Lucy Oliver
Curator

For Advice of Doctor Joseph Milligan,
Medical Superintendent,
Aboriginal Protectorate,
Oyster Cove,
Van Diemen's Land.

Sir,

The office of His Excellency has recently received advice that it is the intention of His Royal Highness, Prince Albert, The Prince Consort, to mount an International Exhibition of Trade to celebrate the Progress of Empire during the reign of Her Majesty, Victoria, Queen of England.

That Exhibition is to be held in London, at Their Majesties' Pleasure, during the month of May, 1851.

In response to the command of Their Majesties, the Governor requests a Presentation of those precious gems known as "Killiecrankie Diamonds"; lately discovered on Flinders Island, Bass Strait; in particular, a specimen of the Green Diamond, which is reported to be the most Desirable.

It is the Express Wish of His Excellency that you, Sir, being the present Keeper of those Aboriginal people recently removed from the settlement at Wybalenna, now choose from among their remnant a party of fit and healthy men to return to the said Island to collect such Diamonds as may be considered worthy to be shown in London for Their Majesties' Pleasure.

Government House, Sydney, this Fourth Day of October, 1849.
By Command of His Excellency,

CSintung

Colonial Secretary.

31

My hand trembled. The story of the green topaz was no myth. The stones had existed. Maybe they still did. Every memory of Flinders came flooding back – its dreadful history; its wild landscape – and now, here was the proof of its greatest mystery, its best kept secret. I read the letter again, my mind racing.

I had heard of Dr Milligan. He had been the medical superintendent at Wybalenna just before it closed, and remained the Government Medical Officer in charge of Aboriginal Welfare, such as it was, after the settlement moved to Oyster Cove. Somewhere, buried in some long-lost

'Crayfish cages at Killiecrankie Bay', watercolour and pastel, G.M.

correspondence, would be his reply to the governor. Had he gathered the natives and returned? Brownrigg's journal said as much. And had they found the green stones as requested? If they had, why weren't they listed in the official catalogue, along with the more common colours? What had become of them, these 'most desirable' of gems?

I knew then that I would return to the island. I was determined to solve the mystery of those diamonds – I admit it – but there was more: I longed for the romance of the place.

Besides, I had painted nothing since I left.

As you have probably gathered, when I make up my mind about something, I move pretty fast. First, I withdrew the little money that I had set aside for a rainy day and bought a one-way ticket to the island. I figured that I had money enough to get by for six months. I would commit myself to art; but if I hadn't accomplished anything – that is, either sold a painting or had one accepted by a gallery in that time – I would put the whole business out of my head forever. I would come home and get a 'real' job.

I picked up a tent and some camping gear at an army surplus sale, let my flat go and finally contacted the Colonial Museum, asking them to proceed with research into Dr Milligan and the likelihood of his expedition to Flinders, giving my forwarding address as care of the post office on the island.

Within a week I was back at Whitemark, standing at the counter of Bowman's store, ready to do business. When Lex Bowman saw me he laughed.

'Couldn't keep away from the place?' he said.

'I want to stay for a while,' I admitted. 'Set up camp near Killiecrankie and get stuck into some painting. But I need that bike again, if it's still available.'

'How long do you want it for?'

I was ready for this. Renting it from him for six months would cost a fortune, at least by my standards. 'I'd like to buy it,' I said. 'How about twenty dollars?'

He was taken aback. 'That was the wife's. Means a lot to me ...' Then a little smile flickered on his lips. 'How about thirty?'

I shook my head. 'Twenty. No more.'

He peered over the counter at my gear. 'You really painting up there?'

He was taking a different tack. I had to be careful. 'Yes,' I said.

'You good at it then? I mean, you're not doin' this modern stuff? You paint a mountain and it looks like a mountain, right?'

'I'd say so.'

He frowned, thinking. Finally he said, 'Tell you what. Twenty bucks it is – but with a painting thrown in. A real nice one I can put up over the counter. How's that?'

I was pleased. I'd been prepared to go as high as twenty-five, but this arrangement was better than money. It gave me an audience, maybe a buyer. I guessed that every tourist on the island came into Bowman's sooner or later, and there sure as hell weren't any souvenirs to take home. 'It's a deal,' I said, and we shook on it.

I set up camp at Castle Rock, Marshall Bay, halfway between Wybalenna and Killiecrankie. I didn't want to get involved with people, not for a while anyway, and this place was isolated, at least 2 kilometres off the road through thick tea-tree scrub. It suited me perfectly.

I spent my first night by an open fire under the stars, wondering what I might achieve and excited by the prospect of being totally free.

In the days that followed I made short forays to the beach, gathering the marvellous debris cast up by the sea: gnarled and twisted driftwood; bones – wonderful, bleached bones of what creatures I couldn't imagine; and the most amazing shells, like whorls of paper-thin porcelain, some a hand-span in diameter, others no bigger than a dollar coin. I sketched all of these things, to loosen up after so many months of producing nothing.

On the fourth or fifth day I decided to take on the landscape, to try to capture the wild sea or the mountains, or Castle Rock itself.

Immediately after breakfast, when the wind was still low, I left the camp and headed for the beach, my easel under my arm, the rest of my gear stowed in my backpack. I had hardly reached the high tide mark when I heard cries coming from the north. I stopped and looked but could make out nothing; the beach appeared to be deserted. Within seconds I heard them again – human, no doubt, yet there was another, high pitched, like an animal screaming in pain or fear. I dropped everything and ran towards them, though I could still see nothing. I suppose I covered 100 metres before I spotted the trouble.

A fresh-water stream flowed into the sea just above my camp. The sand had been washed out, forming a declivity 2 or 3 metres below the level of the beach. I reached the edge and looked down. An old man and a boy were tugging at the bridle of a horse that was stuck in the soft sand, its back legs already sunk to the haunches. I recognised the boy immediately as Aaron Bates.

I was about to jump down but he spotted me and yelled, 'No! Not that way! It's quicksand. You'll sink. Go round. Go round.' He waved his arm to indicate that I should cross higher up, where the sand was firmer. I reached them without any trouble and grabbed the bridle to lend a hand. As I did, Aaron released his grip and, being much lighter than me, waded into the sand to shove from behind, all the while shouting encouragement to the terrified animal. Somehow it broke free and came stumbling out, almost trampling the old man and myself in the process. As for Aaron, he was caught off balance and fell face first into the slop. 'I'm all right,' he called. 'Grab Ruby. Hang on to her!'

At this the man leapt onto the horse's back, stroking its neck and murmuring reassurances. I was about to compliment him on his fitness when I suddenly realised my error: this was no man – this was a woman! Dressed in a man's shorts and a shirt, and with her dark skin and wiry frame, the mistake was easy to make – until I stood away and looked again, then there was no doubt: her steely grey hair was stuffed under a hat, also a man's, but she had the finest features, and the liveliest black eyes, though she was sixty if she was a day.

By the time I had taken this in, Aaron joined me. 'Thanks,' he said, concentrating on shaking off the dripping sand. 'I reckon we would have lost her without you.' As he spoke he looked up. There was a hint of recognition, but he didn't remember me.

I helped him out. 'I'm Geoff Middleton. You're Aaron, aren't you? Aaron Bates. You and your mates were chucking rubbish onto my easel up at Killiecrankie a few months ago, remember?'

His face lit up. 'That's right. You're that artist. You were painting the mountain. But I thought you were going home?'

I explained what I was doing there and he shook his head. 'Geez, I'm glad you turned up. This is my Gran ...'

The woman touched her hat. 'Lizzie Bates,' she said. 'Pleased to meet you. The horse is Ruby.' She leaned forward, patting its shoulder. 'We came down early after shells, but she wandered off when we weren't watching. Come up here after the fresh water, I reckon, and got stuck in the bloody sand. More trouble than they're worth, horses.'

I noticed a bag of shells lying on the sand. They were the porcelain type that I'd been sketching. 'You collect these?' I asked, bending down to look.

'Sure do.' She dismounted, handing the reins to Aaron. 'They're what you call paper nautilus. They wash in anywhere from April to July. I sell them off the island. Make money too, if they're in good nick. But they break easy. See?'

She held up a broken specimen, its outer casing shattered to reveal the whorled interior. 'Pity. They got this little creature lives in them, and if the shell breaks, or a gull pecks it – that's it. The sea can be a cruel place, you know. A cruel place ...'

She tossed the unwanted shell onto the sand and stood up, eyeing me off as she did so. 'So you met Aaron before, hey?'

'Up at Killie, Gran. He's an artist. He was painting the mountain.'

'Is that right? We don't get too many artists over here. Too rough and ready, I reckon. You camped near the rock?'

I told her that I was, and pointed to the spot.

'Well,' she said, hitching her shorts, 'since you done us a good turn helping with Ruby, how would you like to come up the house for dinner?'

'Sure,' I said, 'I'd like that.'

She turned to Aaron. 'What day is it?'

'Saturday.'

'Paper nautilus', acrylic, P.G.

37

'Righto. Make it tomorrow then. Sunday dinner ...,' she checked herself, '... or do you say lunch? Anyway, how about I pick you up on the main road at noon? That suit you?'

It was an invitation I couldn't refuse. Not only that, I hadn't forgotten about the topaz altogether and here was a chance to find out more.

Next morning I wasn't so happy. After I'd left Lizzie and Aaron I'd actually begun some worthwhile work and was keen to get on with it. The interruption for 'dinner' didn't seem such a good idea, but I went along with it. Just before midday I cycled back to the main road and waited. Sure enough they turned up, Lizzie driving a truck that was almost as old as her. What kept it going I'll never know – sheer determination on her part, I think – but I left the bike in the scrub and climbed in. Aaron slid across what remained of the front seat to make room.

Photograph, G.M.

'How far to your place?' I asked.

'Back towards Killiecrankie,' she yelled over the roar of the engine. 'About 12 kilometres. My Stan, rest his soul, picked up a few acres there. A fifty-year lease the government handed out to veterans after the war. I still run some sheep. My son and daughter-in-law used to help – that's Aaron's parents – but we lost them out on the bay five years ago. Pumping for diamonds, they were. Just me and Aaron now. We make do.'

I glanced at Aaron. He was staring straight ahead, his face set. I remembered what the boys had told me about his folks. It seemed cruel to talk about them in front of him, so I let the subject drop.

Lizzie's house – 'shack' would be a better word – was the perfect match for her truck. It was set on a cleared block overlooking the mountain, with the sea beyond, but that was all I could say to recommend it. We pulled up in the yard and Lizzie disappeared inside, saying she had a roast on. I've never seen such a mess. The place was unpainted weatherboard with sheets of corrugated iron nailed on here and there, 'to keep out the wind', Aaron explained. It had a definite lean, and would have fallen over altogether if it hadn't been for an enormous brick chimney that seemed to prop it up. As for the yard, there were tin sheds everywhere and I counted half a dozen car bodies, all sprouting grass and weeds. A junk dealer would have thought it was heaven!

Aaron was happy to act as my tour guide until we were called to eat, and that was when my eyes were really opened.

Lizzie's backyard

Photograph, G.M.

Inside consisted of two tiny bedrooms, a living room and a kitchen that led to a semi-detached bathroom of corrugated iron. We ate at a scrubbed pine table in the kitchen. The food was excellent – lamb with mint sauce and piles of mashed potatoes, 'all home grown', Lizzie assured me – but throughout the meal my eyes kept wandering, taking in the fantastic collection of objects and artifacts that filled the place. There were bits and pieces on the floor, on the walls and on the shelves and dressers. Most of the stuff was maritime hardware, ropes and fishing gear and the like, while the rest came from the sea itself and bore a marked similarity to the things I had gathered from the tideline to sketch.

When we finished eating I left the table to look around. That was when I spotted the mantelpiece. It was a rough-hewn plank, a piece of old decking, I thought, but by the arrangement of the items on it, it was clear that they bore special significance. In the centre were two timber-framed photographs, one of a soldier with a rifle which I took to be Stan, and the other of a man and a woman holding a baby. This had to be Aaron's parents. To the left was a bone china cup and saucer commemorating Queen Victoria's Golden Jubilee, and to the right a scrimshaw, an engraved whale's tooth decorated with the repellent motif of a fanged snake. In amongst these objects were what appeared to be lumps of dull, grey rock.

'That's uncut topaz,' Lizzie said, leaving Aaron to clear the table. 'I used to dive for it once.'

'Sorry?'

She took a piece of the stone and held it to the light. 'Dive. You know, under the water.' She caught me staring and laughed. 'Don't believe me, hey? Aaron can tell you. It's only because of him I don't do it any more. I loved it.'

'It's true,' Aaron called from the kitchen. 'She used to take the syphon hose down and suck the stones up off the bottom. I told her if she didn't cut it out, I'd leave. Crazy, that's what she was. You know she's about a hundred and fifty years old.'

Lizzie made a face at the retreating Aaron, and I asked, 'Did you do well? Did you get any good ones?'

'Good ones? 'Course we bloody didn't. Does it look like we're rolling in money?' Then she turned to the mantelpiece. 'But there's always the green ones. One day ...'

'I've heard of the green ones,' I said, hardly believing she had brought the subject up. 'You believe they exist too?'

'You know what this is?' She picked up the scrimshaw and held it out.

'A scrimshaw,' I said. 'Whalers used to carve them out of bone.'

'Not always whalers. This here was done by my grandfather back in the 1850s. It's a snake. See those eyes? What colour you reckon those eyes are?'

I took it from her. 'Green,' I said. 'A green dye, maybe?'

'Yeah, green. Two proper beauties. The colour of that topaz. It's out there, I know it. All burnin' up inside, like two green eyes.'

'But the snake ..?

'There's snakes on this island, believe me. Killers too. Like I said, my old Pa made this. Billy, his name was, Little Boy Billy they called him. He was a proper blackfella. True. He lived on this island when he was a kid, down there at Wybalenna. But after they cleared the place out, and took his mob away to the main island, he came back with some doctor looking for good stones to send over there ...' She was excited now, and flung her arm wide '... over to the Queen. Poor old Pa. He found something, I reckon. Something big. But he never got back again, see? They didn't want no black man coming here. So he done this up for my dad. Reckoned it was a map, see, but my Dad, he was one for the grog, hopeless he was, and whatever old Pa told him he forgot. So now we got nothing, just this snake with two green eyes. They're the topaz, I betcha – but where, hey? That's the question.'

I was speechless. In the space of a few seconds this woman had told me as much as I had found out in months of research. I was about to ask her more when I realised that Aaron had entered the room, and stood watching us. He was far from happy. He had the same hard look in his eyes that I had noticed when I first met him. 'I reckon Geoff wants to get on with his work now,' was all he said.

Lizzie took the hint. 'You ready?' she asked.

I nodded, taking one last look at the scrimshaw before handing it back. 'That's a remarkable piece of history you've got there,' I said. 'It should be in a museum.' Nobody answered, and throughout the drive back to my camp Aaron said nothing. I thought, oh well, too bad, I came here to paint anyway – but that night I dreamt of snakes and queens in tea cups and galaxies of twinkling green stars.

'Little Boy Billy', Henry Purcell, pencil and china white

Sketch of Luke and Johnno fossicking, pencil, G.M.

The next time the topaz were mentioned was in completely different circumstances. A few days after my visit to Lizzie's, I was sitting outside my tent cleaning brushes when two motorbikes came roaring into camp. I knew right away who it was: Luke and Johnno, Aaron's mates from up at the mountain.

Luke sauntered over, cool as you like. 'We come to see if ya wanted someone to chuck rocks at ya. Do ya? No charge for tourists.'

I laughed. 'How did you know I was here?'

'We met Aaron's grandma at the store,' Johnno explained. 'She told us you pulled Ruby out of the sand and where you were camped. We were just passing, as they say, and thought we'd drop in to see how you were going.'

'Yeah, and we got a message from old man Bowman too. He reckons you owe him a painting. Is that right?'

'Tell him I haven't forgotten. I'm working on it.'

They sat on the sand beside me, fiddling with my paints and brushes. 'So, you done Killie yet?' Luke suddenly asked.

'What?'

Johnno explained a second time. 'He means have you painted the mountain. You know, Killiecrankie?'

'I haven't been up there yet. Take me the best part of a day to get there on my bike. Give me a week or so. I'll break camp here and set up again there. I'll see how I go.'

I noticed that they exchanged glances, apparently negotiating something. I felt vaguely threatened until Johnno said, 'We're going up the mountain now to do a bit of fossicking. You want to come? Luke can take two on his bike.'

'What sort of fossicking?'

Luke shook his head as if to say, 'stupid tourist', but he contained himself. 'Topaz. You know, Killiecrankie diamonds.'

'I thought that was all a deep dark secret. I thought you didn't like outsiders poking around up there. That's the impression I got from ...'

Johnno cut me off. 'From Aaron? Nah. We aren't all like him. He's got a real thing about the diamonds. You'd think they were all his, to listen to him.'

'It's cause of his great grandad. Aaron's an Abo, ya know.'

Luke had said this almost as an aside, but suddenly the truth struck me. 'I never even thought of that. You're right. He is. Lizzie said her grandfather was, so ...'

Johnno gave me a pat on the shoulder. 'You can't tell to look at him, but that's the truth. That's how come he's got this thing about the stones. Specially the green ones, eh Luke?'

His friend had already lost interest. He was heading back to his bike.

Johnno ignored him. 'Look,' he said, 'you need to understand about Aaron. He's a good mate and all, but he's got it into his head that his great grandad – Little Billy or something – actually found these green stones but they got stolen from him, or lost, or something. Anyway, his dad believed the same thing – everyone on the island knows that – and that's how come he died, see, dredging in this deep pocket out in the bay where he reckoned the green ones were. Or came from, or something ...'

He might have told me more if Luke hadn't yelled, 'You comin' or what?'

Johnno gave him the finger but headed for the bikes anyway. I threw a sketchpad and some charcoal into my backpack and within five minutes I was back on the road to Killiecrankie.

I know this sounds crazy, but until that day I'd never really seen the mountain, not properly, at least. The boys took me around the base of it, following a track marked by piles of rocks, little cairns, like in an Indian movie, and all the while the granite cliffs reared up beside us. If I'd had my way we would have stopped every 100 metres, there were so many fantastic outcrops just begging to be explored, but Luke wouldn't wait. Johnno was different. 'It's okay,' he reassured me. 'You can take a breather soon. There's a special place. You'll see.'

That 'soon' was a long time coming, but after a solid hour's walk we came to a headland and Johnno stopped, letting Luke go on alone. 'Down here,' he said, and there, tucked away among the boulders, was a makeshift cabin.

'That's what we call "the hut",' he said, leading me inside. 'It's where people stay overnight if they're seriously looking for diamonds. I mean, for a weekend or something. I thought it might suit you, if you were coming up this way, you know, to paint the mountain, maybe.'

He was right. The place had real possibilities. The situation was perfect, right on a headland with the mountain behind. As for the hut, well, I would have to throw my tent over the frame to make it waterproof, but someone had done a good job of setting up the basic creature comforts of benches and fireplaces and wash-stands and the like.

'Does it get used much?' There seemed little point in staying there if I had to share. That was the last thing I wanted to do.

'Not any more. We used to get lapidary clubs over from Tassie, sometimes even from Melbourne, but that seems to have stopped. You know who does stay here sometimes? Aaron.'

'But he only lives a few kilometres away.'

'It's his grandma. She drives him nuts. Always that stuff about his parents, and "the sea can be cruel".'

'I heard. I thought he had it pretty tough.'

'He does. So he shoots through for a day or two. Ruby keeps him company. But he wouldn't get in your way. Not Aaron. He's not one for people. If he saw you here, he'd say "Hey" and disappear. Anyway, we better catch up with Luke. He'll be down Diamond Gully, where the topaz are. You never know, you might be lucky and pick up something.'

This 'gully' was more of a ravine, funnel-shaped, and littered with boulders. Its bed was thick with gravel, suggesting that a stream had run there once. It was here that the boys taught me to fossick for the topaz. The process was a simple one: drop onto the hands and knees, sort through the gravel with the fingertips – and yell 'I got one' if a likely stone turned up.

Sketch of Ruby at the fossickers' hut at Killie Castle, crayon and watercolour, G.M.

I found two – both small and cloudy – but I was happy. I put them in a container I used to carry my charcoal and treated them as if they were the crown jewels.

It was late afternoon by the time we left, and the boys were eager to get home, but as I stumbled along, careful not to slip and tumble into the sea, Johnno suddenly stopped. 'Look,' he said, pointing upwards. Two stone monoliths appeared to teeter on the very edge of the escarpment, huge oblongs of granite they were, a matching pair, perhaps 30 metres high and half that across, and as the rays of the setting sun struck their surface they shimmered with light, like the pillars of some celestial altar.

THE BEGINNING
◆ OF THE END ◆

'Stackey's Bite, Killiecrankie,' linocut postcard, G.M.

I returned to my camp elated. I wanted to get back to the mountain, to set up a fresh camp there, but there were practicalities to consider. Killiecrankie was a long way from the store at Whitemark and my provisions were running low; second, I was determined to finish a painting for Bowman, not so much to keep him happy but to get a piece of my work on public display. The sooner that was done, the better.

This proved to be a sensible plan. Within a week, just as I was reduced to my last can of beans, I was satisfied that I had something to show: not one, but three finished canvases, all seascapes, and all acceptable to the public eye.

Bowman was delighted. 'Geez,' he said, clearing a space on the wall behind the counter, 'these things are good enough to be on a calendar.' I took this as a compliment, though I'm not sure that my tutor at the Academy would, and then he really made my day. 'Tell you what, I'll swap you one for some tucker. How about ten bucks worth? That sound okay?' Why would I quibble? I'd sold a painting, which was all that mattered.

But that was nothing compared with how I felt when I collected my mail. Buried among the 'wish-we-were-there' letters from friends at home was an envelope from the museum. The Milligan documents had arrived.

Tasmanian Archives
107 Davey Street
Hobart 7000

18 July 1969

Dear Mr Middleton

With reference to your request for documents relating to Dr
Joseph Milligan, Medical Supervisor of Aborigines, Van
Diemen's Land, and an expedition he undertook to Flinders
Island in 1849, I have pleasure in forwarding the following
material:

1.   Letter (dated 20 December 1849) from Dr Milligan to the
      Governor regarding the planned expedition.

2.   Letter (undated) from Dr Milligan to the Governor
      regarding the outcomes of the expedition.

These are the only documents written by Milligan himself about
the expedition that I was able to find. I have, however,
traced 'secondary' references to the expedition which may be
of value to your research, as follows:

1.   A double-sided broadsheet entitled 'Trust Betrayed',
      printed in Hobart and dated 22 April 1850. (Dr Milligan's
      expedition must have been considered big news in Hobart
      Town at that time.)

2.   A map and a series of sketches believed to be by the
      artist Henry Purcell, who accompanied Dr Milligan on the
      Flinders Island expedition as a map maker.

Thank you for your inquiry. I hope that you will find these
materials useful

Best wishes

Peter McDonald
Senior Archivist

"The Larches,"
Battery Point.
20th of December, 1849.

His Excellency, the Governor,
  Sir,
          I am honoured to receive Your letter requesting that I arrange for a party to gather topaz on Flinders Island, such gems to be forwarded to Their Majesties for consideration as examples of the produce of this Colony at the forthcoming Great Exhibition of London.

          As an expression of my willingness to comply with your request, I have chartered a suitable vessel, the "Helen," out of Hobart Town, which will depart that port, with your Excellency's Approval, in one month.

          With regard to Your Excellency's Suggestion that I employ Natives from the Community presently encamped at Oyster Cove, I regret to advise that, because of old age or physical infirmity, such natives as remain in that establishment are incapable of serving Their Majesties in this noble Enterprise. I am able to find only one native who may be considered worthy of use, this being a boy aged but fourteen years, yet who is strong and willing and possessed of considerable intellect. Furthermore, his knowledge of the Island is extensive, since he was in the habit of frequenting the Diamond beds during his time at the Wybalenna Settlement.

          I have also acquired the services of two convicts of the Colony: One, James Gallagher, a Cook, transported for Petty Theft and serving seven years; the other, Henry Purcell, a Map Maker, transported for fourteen years for Forgery. These persons would be invaluable to the success of such a Venture, and all three (both native and felons) have the further advantage of incurring no wages or payment for Services, being dependants of the Empire.

          I again extend my thanks for the privilege of serving Their Majesties.
                    Your obedient servant,
                    Joseph Milligan
          Royal College of Surgeons, Edinburgh,
                    Medical Superintendent,
                    Aboriginal Protectorate,
                    Oyster Cove,
                    Van Diemen's Land.

J. M.
370

48

His Excellency, the Governor,

Sir,

In response to Your Excellency's request that I undertake an Expedition to Flinders Island to gather gems for Their Majesties' Great Exhibition, I am honoured to present the outcomes of that journey.

The success of the Venture is evident in both the quantity and quality of the gems which accompany this correspondence. To wit:

Natural Straw-coloured Topaz:	300 Specimens
Natural Yellow Topaz:	40 Specimens
Natural Pink Topaz:	30 Specimens
Blue Topaz (Possibly Aquamarine)	30 Specimens
Natural Green Topaz (Very Large)	1 Specimen

As it was the express wish of Their Majesties that to receive a "Green Diamond," I draw to Your Excellency's attention that such a Diamond has indeed been procured.

However, my Journey was not without Misadventure. A second Green Diamond, equal in both colour and size to that forwarded, has been lost, under calamitous circumstances.

Although commended to me, the convict James Gallagher proved to be of a poor base nature, and absconded into the Wilderness with this gem. As the weather was poor, and the constraints of time were against us, insofar as we must meet our Vessel on her return journey, the intended recapture of this felon was abandoned.

At Your Excellency's request an account of this calamity will be furnished by my Self, being witness to the Events.

I trust that those gems supplied meet with Your Excellency's approval.

Your Obedient Servant,

Joseph Milligan

Doctor Joseph Milligan,
Medical Superintendent.

J.M.
368

TRUST BETRAYED!

AN ACCOUNT OF THE ABSCONDMENT OF THE FELON, JAMES GALLAGHER WHILE IN THE SERVICE OF THEIR MAJESTIES

DR JOSEPH MILLIGAN, Noted Surgeon of Hobart Town, hereby recounts his Tale of Trust Betrayed while in the Service of His Excellency, the Governor, and Their Royal Majesties.

Dr Milligan has obliged us with the following narrative in his own words:

At the COMMAND OF HIS EXCELLENCY, I was instructed to lead an Expedition to Flinders Island, in order to gather such precious gems as are to be found there-namely the famous 'KILLIECRANKIE DIAMONDS'- and to despatch these for the consideration of Their Majesties, whereupon, such gems would be displayed to the glory of the Empire at the GREAT EXHIBITION OF LONDON, in the month of May, 1851.

Having but little knowledge of the Flinders Wilderness, I gathered about me such persons as I deemed best for the Expedition: a native, variously known as 'Billy Boy', or 'The Boy', and two felons. One, James Gallagher, a Cook, of Ireland, and the other, Henry Purcell, English born, a Map Maker, lately practising as an Artist in the Colony.

I further engaged the services of CAPTAIN WILLIAM OGILVIE, Master of the Schooner, 'HELEN', out of HOBART TOWN, this vessel to carry provisions for the Expedition. Our live cargo included two mares, one being for my personal transport and the other to serve as a pack animal. All this being done with no impediments, the 'Helen' departed Hobart Town, under a fair wind, on the 28th of January.

Our voyage to FLINDERS ISLAND being accomplished in good weather, we disembarked without incident at the Little Harbour, a half mile to the South of Killiecrankie Bay, on the 2nd of February. Captain Ogilvie advised that the 'Helen' would return to collect our party after three nights — that being sufficient time to complete our task — during which interval the Vessel would proceed South to the sealers' settlement at Cape Barren Island.

From the moment of landing, the behaviour of the convict Gallagher was insubordinate and belligerent. This mal-content showing no desire to aid in the establishment of our camp, I exhorted him strongly to Obedience.

The second day we made our way North, following the coast of Killiecrankie Bay, until we encountered the rugged slopes of MOUNT KILLIECRANKIE, where a second camp was established. Gallagher remained insolent during this entire journey, lagging behind, and expressly refusing to carry packs, preferring to load the horses, which were already over extended, or attempting to cajole the boy into being a pack animal. Indeed the native boy would have performed this Duty, had I not interceded to prevent him.

On the second night, a fierce squall struck our camp. We were obliged to seek shelter in Caves nearby, returning in the morning to a scene of devastation. On being ordered to help bring order out of this chaos, Gallagher resorted to threats against my person, and I was obliged to produce my firearm as a means of retaining Command.

After the camp was restored in a more sheltered situation, we commenced our search for the Diamonds. The native boy, once an inhabitant of this Island, was delighted to lead us to the most likely places where the gems might be found. Nor did he deceive us. In the progress of that single day, we located several hundred of the gems, of diverse colours and great worth, including two of the rarest, being deep green in colour!

The temptations of such Riches proved too much for the base creature, Gallagher. That night was our last upon the Island, and again experiencing inclement weather, the horses bolted. In the interval afforded by our search for the animals, the mis-creant Gallagher returned to camp and, under cover of darkness, stole away with all our provisions and Her Majesty's Diamonds.

In pursuit of the Thief, the boy Billy led our party high into the MOUNTAINOUS TERRAIN and this strategy met with some success. Having my quarry once in my sights, I fired upon him, striking him and causing him to cast aside the greater part of his booty, including the Diamonds. These were recovered and returned to myself by the loyal native — save for one: a GREEN DIAMOND of untold worth, which no doubt remained in the Thief's possession.

What next transpired is the GREATEST CALAMITY of all. The condition of the weather continued to worsen, a circumstance which caused me GRAVE ALARM. I espied the 'Helen' entering the wild waters of the Bay, whereupon she was tossed like a cork! I was therefore obliged to arrive at a decision: to proceed with the chase or, in consideration of the welfare of my charges, and likewise of Captain Ogilvie and his crew, to quit the Island before the Vessel was sunk and ourselves cast-away.

This latter I did, abandoning the villain Gallagher to his Fate, and returning without further mis-adventure to Hobart Town.

The villain Gallagher is fired upon

To all who read this Narrative, I say: LEARN THESE LESSONS:

'TRUST NO ONE, FOR MAN IS A CREATURE OF FOLLY' and 'THE DESIRE FOR RICHES IS MAN'S GREATEST CURSE'!

THE CAMP AT
◆ KILLIECRANKIE ◆

I read those documents right there on the post office steps, and then, my mind racing, I peddled back to Marshall Bay. There could be no doubt whatsoever that the green stones existed. I mean, it was impossible to believe otherwise; nobody could have invented such massive and sustained lies. That was the first thing I settled. And then I imagined them there, Milligan and his troupe, laughing and shouting in Diamond Gully as gem after gem turned up. Hell, in those days they must have been lying as thick on the ground as the gravel itself! What's more, if the word was out about the green ones before Billy found his two – and it must have been, if Her Victorian Highness, the Jewel Gatherer of the Empire knew, way over in England – then, were there more? Were they still there, buried in some lost vein, caught up in a crevasse or, as I guessed Aaron's folks believed, washed down into the sea? Beneath all this was the nagging possibility that the second stone could still be there, along with the remains of the unfortunate Gallagher. There was something to dream about!

I was so taken up by all this that I missed a curve and came off the bike. Sitting in the dirt, my head hurting, knees bleeding, surrounded by cans of beans, I came to my senses. What the hell was I thinking? What was I doing? I had sold a painting that day. Sure, I got ten bucks for it, in kind at least, but that was better than some pie-in-the-sky dream of a handful of green diamonds. It was different for Aaron. He had a reason to look for them. It was in his blood, so to speak. To Luke and Johnno it was just a game, the thrill of the hunt. But for me it had become an obsession: a ridiculous obsession. Maybe Milligan was right in his own preachy way: the desire for wealth was man's greatest curse!

Once again I determined to put the jewels out of my head. I had come to the island because I loved the place, because it excited me, because it made me long to paint. That was exactly what I would do – and where I wanted to, not hiding in limbo at Marshall Bay, halfway to my goal. Killiecrankie. That's where I should be.

I broke camp that afternoon, loaded up the bike, and took off. I set up again at 'the hut' and got stuck into painting. When I look back, after all these years, I would have to say that those were the happiest days of my life.

I saw Luke and Johnno from time to time. They would come up unannounced and spend an hour or two just hanging around. Sometimes they would pick up supplies for me from Bowman's, which was great, since it

'The Fangs', oils, G.M.

was a day's ride there and back. I saw Aaron and Lizzie once or twice, either on the road or at the store, though he was up at the mountain, I was certain; I heard a horse at odd times, but only once did I actually see him.

I was drawing in the scrub above the gully and there he was, high in the escarpment, moving among the boulders. I could have called him, but I didn't. He knew where I was if he wanted company.

Approaching summer brought the tourists and little by little my work began to sell. Nobody wanted big stuff, it was the sketches they liked: charcoal, quick watercolours, even coloured pencil. 'Calendar pictures', as Bowman called them; mementos of the island that could be neatly hung on living-room walls. I didn't mind, I was paying my way, but soon I bored even myself.

One evening, desperate to do something worthwhile, I took my gear up the trail to the two great stones that caught the sun. They were as I remembered them: isolated, huge, even menacing. I worked on them for days, producing sketch after sketch, rough after rough, until I was satisfied. I liked what I had done so much that I even knocked up a few smaller versions for sale. Why not? I would keep the original, which was all that mattered.

Next time I went down to Bowman's I took a few of these with me. He stuck them up on the counter and stood back, fancying himself as a connoisseur of my work. 'Interesting,' he said. 'Very interesting. You know what they look like? Two big teeth. No. Fangs. That's it. Snake fangs. See?' He laughed, demonstrating with two fingers. 'But you watch out now, there *are* snakes up there, bad ones too. They come out in summer. Copperheads. Tiger snakes. Real killers. You better watch out ...'

I looked at the paintings again. The stones did look like fangs. Upright. Parallel. And ever so slightly tapered towards the top. The snake on the scrimshaw at Lizzie's place immediately came to mind, and her warning too, but there was something else, some other associated word or image lurking in my mind.

The answer came in the middle of the night – the Milligan documents; there was something about snakes in the Milligan documents, though for the life of me I couldn't recall what it was. I lit my lamp and dragged out the museum envelope, spreading the papers over my makeshift bed. At first I could find nothing, certainly not in print, and then, as I was about to give up, I spotted it. Printed in the most delicate lettering on Henry Purcell's map of Killiecrankie Bay were the words, 'The Fangs', and the tiniest arrow pointing to the very spot were the twin stones stood.

First thing next morning I headed directly for Lizzie's and found her fiddling about in the yard.

'Hello, stranger,' she said, 'come up for dinner again then?' I wasn't too sure of what to say, how to approach what I really wanted, but I accepted her offer of a cup of tea and asked, out of interest, if Aaron was about. 'He's off with Ruby somewhere. I'll probably see him tomorrow.' She disappeared into the kitchen to get the tea.

As soon as she was gone, I went to the mantelpiece and picked up the scrimshaw, determined to examine it properly this time. Certainly the motif of the snake that twined about it demanded attention, but now, as I turned it slowly in my hands, I noticed features – hardly more than scratches on the surface, really – that I had overlooked before: here was a wallaby, dolphins, a boat – and what were these? Huts? Tents?

I was suddenly conscious that I was being watched, and looked up to see Lizzie staring at me.

'You like that, don't you?' she said, putting the tea things on the table.

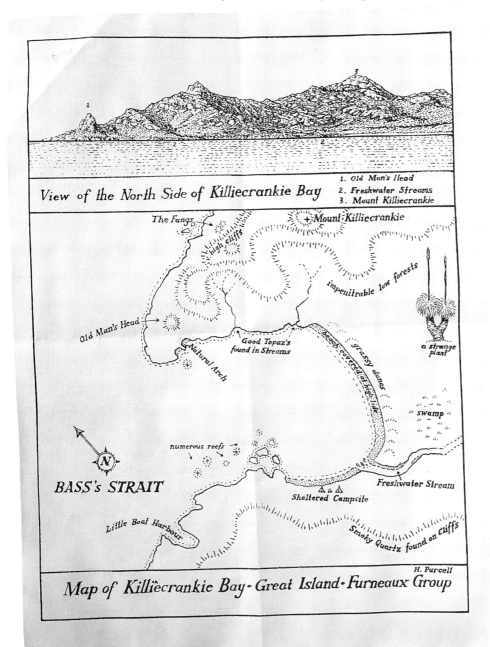

View of the North Side of Killiecrankie Bay

1. Old Man's Head
2. Freshwater Streams
3. Mount Killiecrankie

Map of Killiecrankie Bay · Great Island · Furneaux Group

H. Purcell

'I do,' I said, then, gathering courage, 'Could I borrow it for a while? I'd like to ...'

'No,' she said, and gently, determinedly, she took the scrimshaw from me and replaced it beside the cup on the mantelpiece.

We drank tea and made island small-talk for an hour or so, then I left, feeling cheated. That scrimshaw was more than a piece of folk art. That snake, those fangs, those curious little sketches – if all that didn't mean something, I was a monkey's uncle. But as I thought of these things, I realised something else: the yearning for the topaz had come over me again.

The next few days were very strange. I forced myself to get out, to get on with my work, and yet I sensed that I was not alone. Several times, at first, I stopped painting and looked up, certain that I was being watched. On the second day I actually called out, expecting Luke and Johnno to appear from the scrub, grinning. And then on the third day, I heard the distinctive snuffle of a horse. I knew then who it was, Aaron, and tried to ignore him.

On the fourth day matters finally came to a head. I had worked well all day. I had heard nothing, no horse, no snapping twigs, and for the first time I was convinced that I was alone; that my 'little native companion' had finally found something better to do. What that was, exactly, I was about to find out.

Mid-afternoon, as the sun was still high, I returned to camp hot and tired. I slipped my backpack from my shoulders and was about to get some water when the feeling that I was being watched came over me again. I turned suddenly and there was Ruby, almost right on top of me, and then a movement in the hut caught my eye. I pulled the canvas entry aside.

Aaron was sitting on my bunk with his back to me. He turned when I entered and looked me straight in the eye, at once curious and defiant. It was a look that I remembered well. He had used it on me that first day we met, when he had turned back as the boys rode away. I looked beyond him to see what he was doing. The envelope from the museum had been opened. The Milligan papers lay scattered on the bed. On top of them was Purcell's map, and on top of that, the scrimshaw.

I was speechless, but Aaron seemed unconcerned. 'Watch,' he said, and as I stared, he reached out and picked up the map, rolling it into a cone, keeping the printed side out. Then he held it up. 'See? Now it's a scrimshaw, with a snake curled round it.' He was right. Purcell's perfectly ordinary representation of the coastline was now a spiral, a serpentine line winding about the paper cone. And to prove his point, Aaron held the

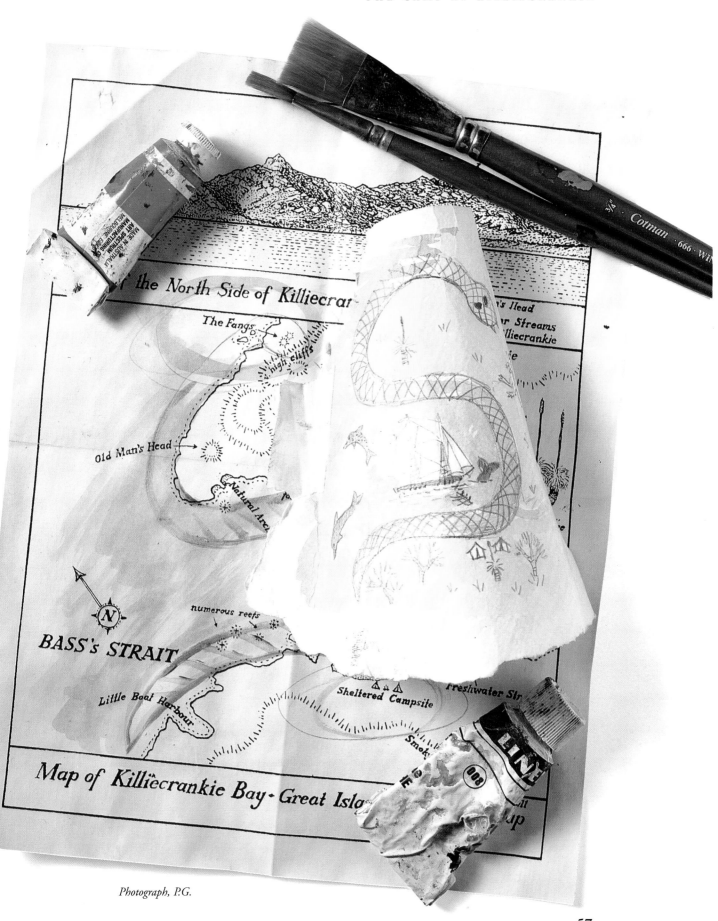

Photograph, P.G.

scrimshaw up beside it. 'See,' he said, smiling, 'that's the secret. The scrimshaw is a map too. But a tricky one. First, Billy must have drawn it like this ...' He released the paper cone, pressing it flat, so that it appeared as a map again, 'and then he curled it around, like this ...' And he wrapped the map around the conical scrimshaw. 'See?'

'Like a template,' I said, sitting on the bed beside him. 'Like cutting a paper template, marking it onto the ivory then engraving it.'

'Yes,' he said.

I couldn't help smiling. 'You knew that I was onto something, didn't you. You've been watching me for days. You've been getting up courage ...'

He dropped his head then lifted it again, suddenly serious. 'Right from the very beginning you wanted the green ones, didn't you? Right from that day with Luke and Johnno. And when you came back and camped up here, and asked about the scrimshaw, I was certain you were looking. Weren't you?'

This was a question I could hardly bring myself to answer. 'What else did you find?' I asked, indicating the documents. 'You've done a pretty good job so far.'

He hesitated a moment, then he picked up the scrimshaw. 'The first thing to do is to see what this looks like out flat. Like the template you said. Like a map.'

He was right. I went out to my pack and returned with paper and a pencil. I took the scrimshaw from him and, starting from an imaginary line through the centre of the snake, began to unfold its coiled image. When the serpent writhed full-length on my sheet, I added the smaller details: the boat, the dolphin, the huts, the wallabies. 'Done,' I said, and held it up. There, without the shadow of a doubt, was a map of Milligan's journey, complete with Captain Ogilvie's vessel, the *Helen*, dolphins leaping in Killiecrankie Bay; huts marking each of the camps – everything was in place. But what did it prove? That was the worry. 'It's no different from Milligan's map,' I said, comparing the two. 'It's just that Billy's was more of a pictogram. A work of art ...'

He looked at the scrimshaw again, turning it towards the light. 'Yes,' he said, 'except you didn't show one bit ...' Then he left the hut.

I followed him out and watched as he knelt by the fire site. He reached down, gathered a handful of the ashes, rubbed them thoroughly into the scrimshaw, then turned to me. 'There,' he said, 'take another look.'

A thin black line now extended from the snake's mouth. It passed midway between the fangs and ended, quite definitely, at a point on the surface of the creature's skin. 'It's a tongue,' I whispered.

Photograph, G.M.

'No,' he corrected, beaming. 'It's an arrow. This is a map, remember. There's something up there, between those Fangs. The lost diamond. You'll see ...'

From the moment he showed me that scrimshaw, Aaron Bates had less than an hour to live.

When you read about someone dying in a novel, or there's a death scene in a movie, you always seem to know that it's coming. There's a sort of drum roll first, so you're waiting. But from my experience, death has no warning. Not in real life. It just happens. Like slipping on a stair. Or cutting yourself with a razor. Or squashing your finger in a cupboard door. That's how low-key death is. And since I'm telling the truth here, trying to face the reality of what happened way back then, it's important that you understand how death came to Aaron. There was no drum roll. No fanfare. Death came simply, from out of the blue.

I have often thought about this.

The Fangs

Photograph, G.M.

Aaron collected the papers and, with Ruby in tow, set out for the Fangs, following a path that led upward through the boulders to the top of the escarpment. We reached the Fangs and passed between them into a ravine, the floor of which was littered with rocks and fallen timber. Aaron tethered Ruby to a twisted root and then we began our search, for what exactly, I wasn't sure. I hardly imagined that the diamond, if it was there at all, was sitting on some velvet cushion waiting for us to find it.

We had gradually drifted apart when Aaron called, 'Over here,' and I made my way to him. He had moved back towards Ruby and stood in a rough semicircle of stones set hard against the cliff face. When I approached he pointed to the ground. 'Someone has been here,' he said, 'and a long, long time ago.'

At his feet lay the remains of a tomahawk, its dull iron head half buried among pebbles, its handle almost entirely rotted away. 'And here.' I followed his gaze. There was a bone-handled knife, its blade hardly more than a sliver of rusted metal.

'Gallagher,' I whispered. 'They have to be Gallagher's. And if it's him, then the diamond ...'

I dropped to my knees and Aaron joined me, sifting through the loose stones and dry, sandy soil. I was certain now that we would find something: a bone, at least, a skull, a rib or two, even the diamond itself. But there was nothing, and having exhausted the limited space, I got up.

Then Aaron cried out. A terrible cry, sharp and urgent. Thinking he had hurt himself I spun around, prepared to help.

How wrong could I have been? He held out to me what looked like a piece of bark or a withered leaf, but as I watched he slipped his fingers inside it and I realised that it was leather – an ancient leather purse. For a fraction of a second his eyes lifted to catch mine, and then he withdrew a jewel the likes of which I will never see again: it filled the palm of his hand like a pool of emerald water and shimmered from within as if lit by a thousand tiny stars. 'This is it,' he said. 'You led me to it.'

I remember reaching out to take the stone from him, but as I did, Ruby suddenly reared, snorting, obviously terrified. We turned together, Aaron and I, and there on the ground was a snake: a sleek, black monster, its vile head raised, poised to attack. Ruby reared again, screaming, and as she did the reins tore free of the root they had been looped around.

I remember a peculiar dry, grinding sound, and one by one the rocks above us began to roll, then fall. The whole episode could not have taken more than a few seconds. There was a noise; the rocks fell; and the dust settled.

I saw Ruby bolt between the Fangs, then turned to Aaron, expecting him to be standing beside me where he had been when the commotion started. I was surprised to see him sitting on the ground, his back against a boulder, an odd smile on his face. 'It was a snake ...' I began, but then I saw his eyes. Glassy, they were, and fixed. I knelt beside him, alternately speaking to him and shaking him. There was no blood, no mark, only the faintest depression on his right temple to suggest that anything at all had happened to him, yet I knew that he was gone, that death had brushed against him and taken him.

That is exactly how I found the lost diamond. And how Aaron Bates died.

At least
his grave
is marked

Aaron's resting place at Wybalenna, photograph, G.M.

❖ A LEGACY ❖

These things happened a long time ago, and while I have tried to put them from my mind – to be free of my shame, my guilt – I have never been able to do so.

You see, I love the island: I love its wild places, its mountains, its history. It has become a part of myself. I have a shack in the hills near Killiecrankie, not far from Lizzie's place. I paint, tourist postcards mostly – not grand gallery art, as I had once hoped – but it's a living, and I never tire of the landscape, nor will I ever leave it.

As for the diamond, that beautiful green stone I glimpsed in Aaron's hand? Lizzie and I returned to Killiecrankie, to the spot where the boy had died, but we never found it. Perhaps it was crushed to powder by the falling boulders, or simply buried beneath them; I will never know. The terrible irony of Aaron's final words is legacy enough for me: 'This is it. You led me to it'.

But that other diamond, the one Milligan sent off to Their Majesties' Great Exhibition? I think I know what became of it, and the price an Empire paid.

'Her Majesty, Queen Victoria, wearing the "Green Fire" diamond', watercolour, Sir Eustace Hawksworth, R.A.